Be sure to look for all the great *McGee and Me!* books and videos at your favorite bookstore.

Episode One:
"The Big Lie"
A great adventure in honesty

Episode Two:
"A Star in the Breaking"
A great adventure in humility

Episode Three:
"The Not-So-Great Escape"
A great adventure in obedience

Episode Four:
"Skate Expectations"
A great adventure in kindness

Episode Five:
"Twister and Shout"
A great adventure in faith

Episode Six:
"Back to the Drawing Board"
A great adventure in dealing with jealousy

Episode Seven:
"Do the Bright Thing"
A great adventure in decision making

Episode Eight:
"Take Me Out of the Ball Game"
A great adventure in putting trust in God

Episode Nine:
"'Twas the Fight Before Christmas"
A great adventure in experiencing God's love

Focus on the Family®

PRESENTS

McGEE™ and me!

'Twas the Fight Before Christmas

Bill Myers

Based upon characters created by Bill Myers and Ken C. Johnson

Tyndale House Publishers, Inc.
Wheaton, Illinois

Finally . . .
for our super-supportive and understanding wives: Brenda, Jean,
Kimberly, Barbara, Cathy, Sue, and the future Mrs. Kenny, wherever
you may be . . .

Front cover illustration copyright © 1990 by Morgan Weistling
Interior illustrations by Nathan Greene, copyright © 1990 by
Tyndale House Publishers, Inc.

Library of Congress Catalog Card Number 90-83520
ISBN 0-8423-4114-5
McGee and Me!, McGee, and *McGee and Me!* logo
are trademarks of Living Bibles International
Copyright © 1990 by Living Bibles International
Printed in the United States of America

98 97 96 95 94 93 92 91 90
9   8   7   6   5   4   3   2   1

Contents

"Don't look to men for help: their greatest leaders fail. . . . But happy is the man who has the God of Jacob as his helper, whose hope is in the Lord his God" (Psalm 146:3, 5-6, *The Living Bible*).

ONE
Major Mishap to the Rescue!

It was a dark and stormy night. Wind blew. Rain poured. Waves crashed. (I'd say that about covers it for dark and stormy nights, wouldn't you?) Everywhere water cascaded upon the shipwrecked survivors. It looked hopeless for them as they desperately clung to the side of their life raft—a life raft that looked suspiciously like a giant soap dish. Suddenly, cutting through the waves, appeared the good and mighty ship S.S. Rubber Ducky!

A cheer sprang from the survivors. They were saved! They would live. Once again they would be free to ponder life's most puzzling questions. Once again they would be free to ask why they had to learn the multiplication tables when everyone and their brother own a pocket calculator. And once again—

But wait! Suddenly from the dark, murky depths swam up the fierce and treacherous sea monster known throughout the world simply as "Wash Cloth." Before Ducky knew what hit him, Cloth surrounded him from underneath, covered him with his thick, nappy hide, and began dragging him to the bottom of the ocean.

"Quack, quack, choke, choke, glug, glug . . . "

The survivors watched in horror as their last hope disappeared into the—

RING . . .

As their last and final hope disappeared into the—

RING . . .

It was the phone. Rats. I hate it when that happens. Nothing destroys a good bathtub fantasy like a telephone call.

RING . . .

All right, already. Hold on to your sea horses.

"Hello," I said. "Clark Cant here."

"Clark?"

I immediately recognized the voice on the other end. It belonged to our beloved leader, the president. "Clark," he repeated. "Do you have a mirror in your room?"

What a stupid question. With my incredible good looks and appreciation of beauty, how could I not have a mirror in the room? Actually in every room. Actually dozens in every room.

I threw a look over to my gorgeous reflection and let out a gasp. Where was my tan? What had happened to my gorgeously bronzed body? All those hours at the tanning salon and for what? All I had to show for it was a body that looked . . . how could it be? . . . but my skin . . . it looked gray! I glanced up to my beautiful baby blues. Double gasp! They were also gray! And my lovely blond locks. Gasp! Gasp! Gasp! Everywhere I looked, everything I saw—it was awful, but everything was a terrible, boring shade of (you guessed it) gray.

"Clark," the president continued. "You need to contact Major Mishap for us. His archrival, the fiendish French freak, Monsieur Mon O. Chrome, is on the loose again. He has stolen all of the world's colors and is holding them hostage inside his giant blimp."

Quicker than you can say "Is it just my imagination or are these McGee tales getting weirder?" I hopped into my Mishap Mobile and raced off. I was looking for the nearest toll booth in which to change. (I prefer a phone booth, but some other superhero owns the franchise on those so I go for the next best thing.) Finding an empty toll booth, I leaped out of my car and was immediately transformed from the mild-mannered Clark Cant into the world-famous crime fighter and acne-free good guy, Major Mishap!

With my cape flapping heroically in the wind, I took a mighty leap and flew into the air. I sailed magnificently—for about three feet before doing a dynamic nose dive into the concrete. My ever-so-keen intellect told me something wasn't quite right. Immediately I checked the batteries in my cape. Hmmm, just as I suspected. My A.C. had gone D.C. through the polarization of my whatchamacallits. (Translation: the only way I was going to get airborne was to find a good plane.)

Fortunately a Hertz Rent-a-Jet just happened to be landing nearby, so I quickly filled out the forms, left the birthright to my firstborn as deposit, pulled back the throttle, and roared into the wild gray yonder.

From high in the sky, things looked worse than I had expected. Without color everything was an awful shade of drab. I mean, it was as boring as your Grandmother's old photo album. No color anywhere . . . just black, white, and gray. It was worse than the first part of "The Wizard of Oz," before Dorothy lands in Munchkinville.

And then I saw it . . .

High overhead was Mon O. Chrome's blimp—its sides bulging from all the colors it was holding prisoner.

My radio crackled to life. "So you've finally found me?"

It was Mon O. Chrome. There was no mistaking it. His voice was as boring as everything else about him. Poor guy. Even his autobiography, My Greatest Most Super-Keen Adventures of All Times, was a bore. In fact, it was so boring that doctors around the world prescribed it to patients who couldn't sleep. "Just read two of these paragraphs, and call me in the morning," they'd say.

And it always worked!

So now, Monsieur Mon O. was set on making the rest of the world as boring as he was.

"Mon O.," I called through the radio, "You haven't got a chance. Give up while there's still time."

But instead of an answer he began growling and barking. That's right . . . growling and barking.

Well, you didn't have to be a rocket scientist to figure out what that meant. The man obviously wanted (here it comes) a "dog fight." (Look, I

12

warned you.) That was fine with me. If he wanted to battle it out in the skies, we'd battle it out in the skies.

But before I had a chance to form one of my fabulous plans, he threw his blimp into hyperboogie and came at me with his guns a-blazing.

Fortunately, because of my incredible flying skills (not to mention my dashing good looks), I was able to outmaneuver him. In fact, my skills were so great that as I zoomed past him I could see the poor guy already turning gray with envy.

"Mon O.," I tried to reason. "Give it up. This is your last warning."

No answer. Instead he pulled up, shot high over my head, opened up his bomb bay doors, and began dropping water balloons. Only instead of water, they were filled with paint. Awful drab colors of gray and black.

Ker-Splash, Ker-Splosh, KER-SPLAT!

It was the "Ker-splat" that got me. And it got me good. Right across the ol' windshield. I was blinded. I couldn't see a thing. Before I knew it, my plane dipped into a steep dive and began falling, out of control. I fought to pull it back up. But since I had no idea where up was, I wasn't as successful as I could have been.

"NICHOLAS!" I shouted.

It's not like I was scared or anything. But we cartoon characters always call out to our creators when we're about to be destroyed, pulverized, and/or smashed to bits. I think it's a law or something. And, always being one to obey the law . . .

"N I C H O L A S ! ! !"

But Nicholas was nowhere to be found. I had no alternative. Without a word I did the most heroic thing possible. I bailed. Before you could say "Hey, it's been real, I've had a great time, but now I gotta go," I reached down and pressed the ol' Eject Button.

K-SWOOOOOOOOSHHHHHHH!

I shot out of that cockpit faster than kids out of a classroom the last day of school. Higher and higher I flew. Right past the blimp and the laughing Monsieur Mon O.

I pulled my ripcord and watched as my parachute opened up. Gently I began floating back down. Now, normally the game would have been up. Normally ol' Mon O. boy would have won. But since I'm supposed to be the superhero in this story and since my name's on the cover of this book . . . well, what other choice did I have? I'm supposed to win, right? It's in my contract.

So, of course, a brilliant thought flashed through my mind. I reached into my backpack and pulled out my steel-cleated golf shoes—the very shoes I carry for just such occasions. Quickly, I slipped them on.

The blimp was right below me. I carefully maneuvered my parachute until my steel cleats landed right smack dab in the center of the overstuffed balloon. And, sure enough . . .

K-BLAM!

I ripped a hole in that puppy the size of Pinocchio's nose on a good day of lying. Before ol' Mon O. knew what had hit him, he was zipping back and forth across the sky, completely out of control.

SWIIIISH! SWOOOSH! SWAAAASH!

Colors were spurting out of my custom-designed opening and going in all directions. It was a sight to behold as the colors fell back to earth, replacing all those ugly blacks and grays with their true hues. Once again the Golden Gate Bridge turned golden. Once again the blue skies of Montana turned blue. And once again Detroit turned . . . well, Detroit's always been gray. But, hey, two out of three ain't bad.

Yes-siree-bob. Another dramatic drama dramatically done by the one and only—Tum-Da-Da—Major Mishap.

Now if I can just get back to my bath and Yellow Ducky before the bubbles are all gone . . .

TWO
The Tragic Pageant

While McGee was inside Nicholas's sketch pad enjoying his fantasy as Major Mishap, Nicholas was undergoing his own fantasy. Well, really it was more of a nightmare than a fantasy. At the moment, he was rehearsing for the annual Eastfield Elementary School Christmas Pageant. No problem there. Nick loved being in the pageant. The problem lay in the fact that there were only three days left before the show. The cast and crew needed a little more time than three days. Actually, they needed a lot more time than three days. Actually, the way this pageant was going they could have used three years.

In short, the show was awful!

First, there was the Santa Claus—played by Philip. Nice guy, Philip. Ever since Nicholas had offered to skateboard against Derrick Cryder on Philip's behalf, they had been good friends. No doubt about it, Philip was a good kid. The only problem was this kid didn't know beans about acting. So instead of his Santa Claus giving a mighty "Ho-Ho-Ho!" Philip's version came out sounding a little more like "Squeak-Squeak-Squeak."

Now, to be fair, Philip's acting wasn't the main problem. The fact is, his squeaks had more to do with his size than his talent. I mean, this guy was so small he looked like he had to hop out of the bathtub before draining it just so he wouldn't get sucked under. But everyone figured with enough stuffing and pillows he'd make an OK Santa. Unfortunately, the weight of all that stuffing and those pillows kept toppling him over . . . usually right onto his face. Poor guy. It was all he could do just to keep his balance, let alone deliver his lines.

So, instead of a Jolly Old Elf, this Santa looked like a Tipsy Old Munchkin as he stumbled, staggered, and squeaked.

Not a pleasant sight.

Even so, it wasn't as bad as the dancing snowflakes. Again, it probably wasn't their fault that the record they were practicing to kept skipping. It wasn't their fault that it kept repeating the same three notes over and over again. It wasn't their fault that in trying to keep up with it they were dancing themselves into a frenzied state of oblivion.

Normally Mrs. Harmon would have been there to unstick the needle, but at the moment she was trying to reason with someone playing a shepherdess. The girl kept insisting that her little kitten needed to be in the show, that she would make a great lamb . . .

"Oh, pleeease, Mrs. Harmon. This could be

Fluffy's big break. She loves show business and she won't be any trouble."

Mrs. Harmon threw a doubtful glance at Brutus—a giant St. Bernard who was already having a major barking attack, all because of little Fluffy. Brutus's master was trying to stick some cardboard antlers on his head so he would pass as a reindeer. But old Brutus wasn't interested in being a reindeer. He was interested in being a dog—a dog that barks at, chases, and maybe even eats, cats.

Somewhere amidst all this craziness our young hero, Nicholas Martin, stood, buried under a bathrobe seven sizes too big and a giant, oversized turban that kept falling into his face. Nicholas, Louis, and Derrick had been chosen to play the three wise men. No problem there. Of course, wise men need to wear beards. Still no problem. The problem was that only two out of the three wise men's beards were sticking to their faces. And since Nick was never the luckiest of persons, well, you can imagine whose beard was not staying up.

"It's not going to stick," he kept complaining to older sister Sarah.

But older sister Sarah, who was chomping away on about twelve sticks of Juicy Fruit, would not take no for an answer. She was almost fifteen. She knew how to handle these types of things. She knew how to handle everything.

At the other end of the stage, Mrs. Harmon finally managed to reach the record player. With an awful "ZIPPPPPPP" she lifted the needle, scraping it across every groove of the record.

Everyone groaned and cringed.

But Mrs. Harmon paid no attention. "All right," she called, clapping her hands. "I need all the snowflakes over here, please. All the snowflakes."

By now the snowflakes were so dizzy from dancing to the skipping record that they could barely stay on their feet as they staggered toward her.

Meanwhile, Derrick couldn't resist the temptation to throw a jab in Nicholas's direction. "Hear that, Martin. She wants all the 'flakes' over there."

Nick turned to fire off a nifty comeback, but his head was suddenly yanked around by Sarah. "Will you hold still!" she ordered as she continued to work on the beard. By now she was snapping her gum like there was no tomorrow.

Not far away Renee—good ol' fashion-conscious, every-hair-in-place Renee—was going through her own struggle. She'd been chosen to play the donkey. Not her idea of a great role, but she went along with it. She even agreed to get in the bottom half of the costume, the part with the tail and hoofs and everything. Of course, that didn't mean she wouldn't complain. I mean, after all, she was Renee.

"Look at the waistline on this thing," she whined. "I've heard of the baggy look, but this is ridiculous!"

Now if that had been her only problem, Renee probably would have survived. But it was the giant papier-mâché donkey head coming her way that really ruined her day. "Hold it," she protested. "No way am I wearing that. I just spent $79.95 on a perm and I'm not going to hide it under some—"

But she was too late. Before she could finish her

sentence, Louis's mom had plopped it on top of her head.

After a moment, Renee cleared her throat. "You sure Tina Turner started out this way?" she said, her voice echoing inside the hollow head.

"Trust me," Louis's mom answered.

Meanwhile, our little Santa was walking toward Mrs. Harmon. Well, walking may not be the right word. It was more like stumbling and falling, and stumbling and falling, and stumbling and falling. He was making pretty good progress, though. That is, until he finally arrived . . . and realized he couldn't stop.

Before he could warn the unsuspecting snow-flakes . . .

OOAAFF! BUMP! BANG! He crashed head-on into the first flake, and snowflake number one, still tipsy from her dance with the skipping record, fell face first into snowflake number two, who top-pled into snowflake number three, who . . . well, I think you get the picture. It was like a giant row of dominoes as all six snowflakes fell into each other and tumbled down to the floor.

It was a sight to behold. A work of art. That is, until Brutus leaped into the pile and began licking every face he could get his wet, slobbery, tongue on.

"Ick! Cough! Gag!" the girls cried.

"Bark! Bark! Bark!" Brutus replied.

"Heel, Brutus, heel!" the owner cried.

But no matter how hard the owner pulled or how hard the snowflakes pushed, Brutus just kept coming in for more licks. To him it was a fun, free-for-all game of Pig Pile. To the girls it was a fight for their lives as they kicked and squirmed to avoid the attack of the slurping tongue.

The rest of the cast crowded around for a better look. Soon everyone was having a good laugh. Well, almost everyone. It's not that Mrs. Harmon wasn't having fun. But somewhere underneath that smile there was the look of panic. She knew they had only three days left . . . and she was beginning to hope she could find a less stressful job—maybe as an air traffic controller.

Things were looking brighter for Sarah. In a flash of inspiration she had the solution to Nick's problem. As his beard fell from his chin for the zillionth time, Sarah suddenly spit out her gum, plopped it on the furry hair piece, and quickly stuck it to his chin. Bingo! A perfect solution!

Well, almost perfect. The sick look on Nick's face said it wasn't quite what he'd had in mind. But before he had a chance to complain, McGee suddenly showed up . . .

Yes-siree-bob, leave it to my intense intellectual intelligence to figure that Nicky boy and the gang needed a little help. And since "help" is my middle name— along, of course with "humble," "heroic," "handsome," and . . . (did I say "humble?"), well, I had no choice but to save the day. Now, to say that their show was a complete disaster probably isn't fair. It would be fair to say that if they were really lucky the world might come to an end before opening night.

So without speaking another word, a tremendous sacrifice on my part, I leaped from Nick's notebook and began doing my voice exercises.

"Why voice exercises?" you're asking. Well, my dear reader, that's elementary. As the world's greatest actor with the world's greatest voice, I have to take care of that voice by warming it up. Particularly if I am going to give another one of my world-famous, show-stopping performances.

Yes, it was I, the Magnificent McGee—watched and admired by millions . . . well, all right, watched and admired by thousands . . . hundreds? . . . OK, so Mom and Dad thought I wasn't half bad and agreed to watch me on Sunday afternoons, if I paid them a buck fifty apiece and if there was nothing on TV.

Anyways, I grabbed my spray bottle, hopped onto a nearby ladder, and began warming up with my favorite voice exercise. I'm not sure why it's my favorite. Maybe it has something to do with the lyrics . . .

"Me-Me-Me-Me-Me-Me-Me."

Oh, how I love those words.

"Me-Me-Me-Me-Me-Me-Me."

Such meaning, such depth. . . .

"Me-Me-Me—"

Just then the phone rang. No doubt it was the famous film director, Steven Spellbound. Either that, or his good buddy George Mucus. Poor guys. No matter how many times I tell them I'm not interested in starring in their next flicks, they just keep on asking.

I picked up the phone and answered, "Hey, babe, sweetheart, buddy boy, love ya, you're magic, don't ever change, let's do lunch." (That's Hollywoodese for "Hello.")

It wasn't Steven. Or even George. Instead, it was

William Shakesfear. He wanted me to star in some newfangled play of his called Macbeth. I told him if he changed the spelling of the last half of the title from "Beth" to "Gee" we might have a deal. But only after I saved my little buddy's show.

With that, I grabbed my favorite pair of solar-powered angel wings, slipped them on, and began practicing my part. With a hefty clearing of my throat and a wonderful tenor to my voice, I began: "McGee . . . or not McGee. That is the question."

Almost immediately Nick spotted me and asked in his kindest, most sympathetic voice, "McGee, what do you think you're doing?"

(That's what I like about Nicholas. He's never one to let his sentimentality get out of hand.)

"Why, I'm practicing my part," I explained.

"Part?" he asked. "Your part as who?"

"Why, as Hark," I answered.

"Hark?" he challenged.

"Yeah, you know . . . 'Hark, the Herald Angel'?"

But before Nick could fall down laughing over my wonderful wit, somebody suddenly grabbed the ladder I was standing on and started to walk off.

"Woooaaaaahhhhhhh!" I shouted as I lost my balance and started to fall.

Nick cringed and waited for the crash. But nothing happened. Instead, when he finally opened his eyes, he saw me giving those solar-powered angel wings a pretty good workout. What can I say? The fact of the matter is that I am a great flyer. First I flew past him right side up. Then upside down. Next I tried the Australian crawl, then finally the ever-popular backstroke.

24

"A piece of cake," I bragged as I fluttered effortlessly to the ground. "Pretty impressive, huh?"

But before Nicholas could voice his overwhelming admiration, some stagehand's size thirteen construction boot crashed down on top of me, flattening me flatter than a flannelgraph flapjack.

Nicholas tried his best to ease my pain with a little humor. "Yeah, McGee, I guess you could say you were a real smash."

"Mo, Mo," I mumbled through my flattened mouth. "Mery munny . . . mery munny."

Before Nicholas could show me any more of his underwhelming sympathy and concern, the giant turban on his head fell completely over his face.

"That's great, Squid," a sarcastic voice commented. I looked around to find the source of the sarcasm. It was Derrick Cryder, the all-American bad egg. He and Louis were walking toward us. "The more of your face you cover with that turban," Cryder continued, "the better you look."

Now it's true, Derrick was never the happiest of hoods . . . unless of course he happened to be beating somebody up. But today he seemed even more unhappy than usual.

"Hey, Derrick," Louis countered. "Why aren't you wearing your hat thing?"

"Get outta here! You morons think I'm actually gonna do this junk!" Derrick had such a gentle way with words. "You two clowns will be the only guys standing here Christmas Eve when the curtain goes up."

Unfortunately, Derrick didn't see Mrs. Harmon approaching. Even more unfortunately, her nerves were so fried she was even grouchier than Derrick. "The script calls for three wise men," she growled. "And come Friday, Mr. Cryder, three wise men is what we'll have."

Derrick spun around, a snappy comeback ready to fly. But Mrs. H. wasn't finished.

"Unless, of course, you want to be the first person in the history of Eastfield to take my class three years in a row."

Derrick was speechless. Mrs. Harmon was a teacher. A role model. She was supposed to play fair. But this . . . "This . . . this is blackmail!" he finally sputtered.

"That's right," she said as she headed backstage, grinning like she was suddenly feeling better. "Merry Christmas."

Derrick just stood there staring.

The kids chuckled.

Derrick glared.

And I coughed. Actually, I coughed a lot of coughs—anything to get ol' Nicky boy's attention so he could start scraping me off the floor.

THREE
The Gift of the Magi

By the time rehearsal was over, it was already getting dark outside. That was one of the nice things about Christmastime in Eastfield. Each day the sun seemed to set just a little earlier. And with each setting sun, peace and calm seemed to creep over the city. People buttoned up their coats just a little tighter, parents inched up their car heaters just a little warmer, children snuggled up to fireplaces and heating grates just a little closer. In short, each day as Christmas approached, everything became just a little bit cozier.

Nicholas loved this time of day—right after sunset but just before night. It was a magical time. A time when there was no sun but still plenty of light. A time of stillness, when everyone's work for the day was over. A time when a person could really slow down and think about stuff.

On this particular day there was something that made the time even more special . . .

It was snowing.

It had started late that morning and continued all through the afternoon. It wasn't a heavy snow. It was in no hurry to throw its weight around and try to change the world. Instead, it was a gentle snow. A quiet snow. A snow that came down slow and easy, softening the hard corners of the city, blurring the sharp edges of wire fences and rusty fire escapes until they were buried under a sparkling blanket. A snow that slowly covered the dirt and grime of streets, and turned them into mystical paths of whiteness.

It was as if the weather knew Jesus' birthday was coming—and that his birthday was the chance for the world once again to be made clean and fresh and pure.

Nicholas felt all these things, but somehow he couldn't put them into words . . . not yet. Maybe later when he became a painter or writer or poet or something. But for right now all he knew was that the falling snow, the fading light, and the twinkling Christmas decorations in the store windows were all so perfect that it practically made his chest ache with pleasure.

And he expressed that pleasure the way any red-blooded kid would express it: he shuffled through the snow, slid across icy spots on sidewalks, and fired off the obligatory snowballs at Louis. Normally the two wouldn't be this far downtown, but Nicholas had something very special he wanted to show his buddy.

At first the gift shop didn't look like much—just a little hole in the wall whose window was filled with the usual Christmas stuff. But once the bell jingled and the boys stepped inside . . . well, it was like a miniature wonderland overflowing with old-fashioned Christmas gifts. Wooden rocking horses, gingham dolls, a thousand burning candles all giving off different scents, antique tree ornaments, wooden flutes, nutcracker soldiers as big as men or as tiny as thimbles, electric trains that chugged and whistled all over the shop . . . and the list went on and on and on.

But none of that interested Nicholas. What really interested him was the glass display case directly in front of where he and Louis stood. Without a word Nick stooped down to the lowest shelf. Louis joined him.

There, right in front of them, was the most beautiful music box they had ever seen. Its beauty wasn't in fancy silver, gold inlays, or glittery pearl ornaments. Its beauty lay in its gentle, hand-carved simplicity.

A kindly old shopkeeper approached the boys from behind the counter. Nicholas looked up to her and gave a smile. She returned it generously, catching a glint of candlelight in her eyes. Nick and the old lady had slowly become good friends. Each day for nearly two weeks Nick had swung by the shop to check on the music box. And each day for two weeks the box had lain there unpurchased. In just a couple more days Nicholas would save up enough allowance to finally buy it. And in just a couple more days his mom would have the best Christmas gift she had ever received.

Without a word, the old lady carefully lifted the box from the display case and delicately set it on the counter. The boys rose to their feet and continued to stare.

It was magnificent.

Nicholas reached out and gently opened its lid. It softly began to chime a beautiful and haunting melody—"Carol of the Bells."

"That's Mom's favorite Christmas carol," Nick whispered.

Louis nodded in silent awe. He could understand why. Time seemed to stand still as all three faces, bathed in flickering candlelight, watched and listened.

Suddenly there was a loud "CRASH!" Nicholas and Louis spun around to see three larger boys hop over a broken oil lamp and race toward the door. The oldest-looking boy was stuffing something inside his leather coat.

"You there! Stop! Stop, I say!" It was the shopkeeper's husband. He had spotted them from the back and began chasing after them. But his age was no match for their youth.

Then Nicholas saw something that took his breath away. One of the three boys, the smallest, was Derrick Cryder!

"Stop! Thieves!" The old man continued the chase as each of the boys jostled past Nicholas and Louis on their way out the door. But for just a moment Nick's and Derrick's eyes connected, and for just a moment Nicholas saw something he had never seen in Derrick before . . . fear.

"STOP!"

Then they were gone. Out the door and down the street.

Nicholas and Louis looked at each other. Suddenly the store seemed to have lost its magic. The music carried no joy. Two of those kids—those thieves—were hoods old enough to be out of high school. And Derrick Cryder was with them.

But that didn't bother Nick as much as the look he had seen in Derrick's eyes. It had lasted only a split second—but in that split second Nick could have sworn Derrick's eyes seemed to shout, "Help me . . . I don't want to be here! I'm in over my head!"

Still, it wasn't Nick's business. I mean, he couldn't stand Derrick anyway. And Derrick certainly couldn't stand him. So it was Derrick's problem, not his.

At least that's what Nick wanted to think.

But from that moment on, something began to eat at Nicholas. He wasn't sure what it was or why it was there. But for whatever reason, Nicholas Martin could not put Derrick out of his mind.

Later that evening Nicholas's family celebrated their annual tree decorating time. Well, it was supposed to be tree decorating. But by the way Dad had tangled himself up in all the lights it looked more like Dad decorating. Sarah put it best when she referred to him as "the living Christmas tree."

"Hey, laugh all you want," he answered as he tried to fight his way through the cobweb of wires. "But as soon as I find the loose bulb on this puppy, you're all gonna need some shades."

Yeah, yeah, yeah, save the false bravado for someone who really knows how to bravado. Yes, it is I,

Thomas McGee Edison, world-famous electrician and Oreo cookie connoisseur. Mr. Dad might look like he was fixing the lights, but I was the one who was really saving the day. I was engaging my incredibly ingenious electrical intelligence on the light bulb problem when ol' Nicky boy spotted me at the base of the tree.

"Hey," he whispered. "You'd better be careful."

Careful, schmareful. I appreciate his concern but he obviously doesn't know whom he's addressing. "No pro-blem-o," I answered. "What ya got here is a fused scattafrants with a polynine skrail blatz."

"That's what I was gonna say," Nick said, trying his best to sound intelligent. Poor kid. Sometimes I feel sorry for him having to fake intelligence just to remain in my genius-like presence. But I guess that's the price you pay for hanging out with brilliance.

Still, being the sucker I am for intellectually underdeveloped folk, I let Nick take a gander over my shoulder. "I just reverse the gyro-stabilizers," I explained, "and connect them to these thinga-whatcha-majabbers, and . . . "

With one swift move I reached into the light socket and—

ZZZZZZZZZ-BLUUUUUUEEEEIIIIEEE!

Unfortunately, it wasn't the light bulb that lit up. It was me! Talk about an electrifying experience! I was shocked! In more ways than one. In fact, if ol' Nicky boy hadn't pulled the plug I could have ended up with the most permanent poodle perm you've ever seen!

Fortunately I suffered no side effects from my

enlightening experience. Well, almost none. When-
ever I enter a room there's still the minor problem of
light bulbs lighting up, automatic garage doors
opening, and the channels on remote control TVs
switching. But that's a small price to pay. Besides,
it could just be because of my charged-up personality.

As McGee was once again delighting in his own
greatness, Grandma swooped in from the kitchen
with a tray of Christmas cookies.

"All right!" everyone shouted as they headed for
the tray.

Well, almost everyone. It seems Dad was still a
little tied up.

But his persistence paid off. Finally finding the
missing bulb he shouted, "Here it is! OK, everybody,
get ready. We're talking serious light show, now!"

Everyone stopped and turned. Somehow they
suspected the worst. They loved and respected
Dad. In fact, it seemed that everyone who knew
him loved and respected him. He was a great guy,
a great father, a great husband, and a great man of
God. Unfortunately, he was not a great handyman.

With dramatic flair, he shoved the Christmas
bulb into the socket. And with an equally dramatic
flair, every light in the house went out.

The family groaned in unison.

"All right, not to worry," Dad called as he tried to
fight his way through the wires. "I'll get the fuses.
It will only take a—"

"No, don't, David." It was Mom. "This is kind of
nice this way. You know, with the firelight and
everything."

"Uh . . . right," Dad said, nervously clearing his throat. "I, uh, I planned it this way."

Of course everyone gave him a look and threw in another groan for good measure. And of course Dad pretended not to notice. I mean, after all, it was Christmas. If a guy couldn't get some slack from his family this time of year, when could he? "Here, Daddy," Sarah said as she handed him some popcorn. "Why don't you help me string these."

Dad looked dubiously at the tiny kernels of corn, the huge needle, and (most of all) the ultra sharp point at the end of the huge needle. But, being a man of extreme faith, he figured he'd give it a shot. "Sure," he said with a shrug, trying to remain casual. "Why not."

The family could have thought of a million why nots, but hey, it was Christmas. If a guy couldn't get some slack from his family this time of year, when could he?

As Grandma sat beside Mom on the sofa she couldn't help commenting, "This is exactly how I remember Christmas as a little girl."

"No kidding?" Mom asked.

"Sure. The family all together, no electricity, just the light from the fire . . . " Then with a twinkle she added, "And popcorn fresh from the microwave."

Everyone gave a quiet chuckle. Well, almost everyone. Little sister Jamie was so intent on setting up the miniature nativity scene that she barely heard what the others were saying.

And then there was Nick. Try as he might, he just couldn't shake what he had seen in the store a few hours earlier. Oh sure, he was wrapping presents, decorating the tree, and laughing with everyone else. But that was on the outside. On the inside, he was still thinking about Derrick Cryder. And on the inside, he kept seeing that look of fear in Derrick's eyes.

Mom was the first to notice his mood. And, being the true-blue Mom that she is, she wanted to know what was going on. "Hey," she said quietly. "What's up?"

And Nick, being the true-blue kid that he is, gave the typical true-blue kid answer. "Nothin'."

Mom knew there was always something behind Nick's "nothin's," so she waited for more. Finally Nick continued.

"It's just kinda funny . . . " His voice trailed off for a second as he tried to piece his thoughts together. "Christmas is such a great time of year. Everywhere you look you can see, you know, people celebrating Christmas and stuff."

Mom nodded. So far, so good. But she knew there was more, and her continued silence asked, "So what's the problem?"

Nicholas knew what she wanted to know. So, after a long sigh, he continued. "It's just too bad everyone can't . . . enjoy it."

"But they can, honey," she gently corrected. "You know that. Christmas is what God's love is all about. Everyone can experience it."

Nicholas slowly looked up at her. That's what he had heard all his life. But that's not what he had seen that afternoon. In Derrick Cryder's eyes he saw nothing but hate and fear. He saw somebody who had no idea about God's love.

Mom kept insisting. "God's love is for everyone." She spotted the figures in Jamie's nativity scene and motioned toward them. "Everyone from poor ragged shepherds to rich and powerful kings . . . to conniving thieves."

The last word shot into Nicholas's heart like an arrow. "Thieves?" he croaked. Once again he pictured the look in Derrick Cryder's eyes.

"Well, sure," Mom answered. "Remember the thief on the cross? How Jesus loved and forgave him?"

Nick's head began to spin. He knew God was supposed to love and forgive those who asked. He'd heard it a billion times . . . in church, in Sunday school, everywhere. But Derrick Cryder? The all-school hood? Derrick Cryder, the creepy bully who beat up everyone? Derrick Cryder, the . . . thief? A part of Nick knew it was supposed to be true. But a bigger part doubted it. A bigger part seemed to think Derrick was the exception—that even God could never love Derrick Cryder.

Before Nick could put all these thoughts into words, he was interrupted by a panicked little sister.

"Mom?" Jamie cried.

"What's the problem, hon?"

Desperately Jamie was plowing through the box where the nativity characters had been packed. "I can't find the third wise man . . . I can't find him anywhere!"

"Oh, I'm sure he's in here somewhere," Mom said as she turned to comfort her.

Mom's comforting words did no good. By now little Jamie's chin was beginning to tremble and her voice was sounding nervous and unsteady.

"Maybe . . . " she swallowed hard to fight back the emotion. "Maybe he's . . . lost."

For the second time that evening Nick's heart felt as though it had suddenly been shot with an arrow. What about the third wise man in his pageant? Was he lost, too . . . ?

FOUR

Just When You Thought It Was Safe to Get Back on the Stage . . .

"Maybe I could sign up for the next dog sled expedition to Antarctica. Or join a prison chain gang . . . or . . . or . . ." Mrs. Harmon muttered to herself, trying to think of some way to relax after directing this pageant. Something easier. Something peaceful.

"OK, Philip," she said, clapping her hands. "Let's try it one more time."

She'd said "one more time" about fifty times now. No matter how many times he tried, the tiny Santa just couldn't get out those Ho-Ho-Hos.

Then there was Brutus. The giant dog had been on his best behavior. He'd been the perfect gentleman as they stuck the cardboard antlers onto his head. He'd been the model of obedience as they hooked him to the red wagon that was supposed to be Santa's sleigh.

Yes sir, everyone was proud of Brutus. Well,

everyone but Fluffy, the little kitten that wanted to break into show biz. Every chance she got, cute little Fluffy would meow or growl or hiss at Brutus—anything she could think of to rile the poor guy. But Brutus was smarter than that. No way was he falling for any dumb old cat trick. The only problem was, Fluffy wasn't just any dumb old cat . . .

Meanwhile, backstage, Louis got to be the bearer of some good tidings. "Hey, Nick," he called as he approached his friend. They were both dressed in their wise-man costumes (complete, of course, with sagging beards). But right now there were only two wise men. As promised, Derrick Cryder didn't show up. Now normally not having Derrick around would have brightened up Nicholas's day. But not after last night. Not after his talk with Mom. Not after he began to suspect that Derrick was in real trouble.

"Good news, Bud," Louis continued. "Mrs. Harmon says we can bag the beards."

Nick grinned. It looked like rehearsal finally was starting to go right. Unfortunately, as he soon found out, looks can be deceiving.

"All right, let's try it one more time, Philip." Mrs. Harmon's voice sounded flat and dull, like she was on automatic pilot—like she really wasn't there. Maybe she wasn't.

Up on stage, the little Santa took a deep breath, stepped back into Brutus's wagon/sleigh, and tried again. Around him all the other children were dressed as snowflakes, snowmen, Christmas gifts, Christmas trees, you name it—if it had something to do with Christmas, chances are somebody was dressed like it. Not only were they dressed like it, but they were standing around bored out of their minds. Even Brutus gave a loud yawn as he waited for Take 607 to begin.

But there was one critter who wasn't bored.

You guessed it: Fluffy.

Fluffy had a plan. That's right—cute, little, adorable, innocent Fluffy was about to add more than a little spice to the rehearsal.

Philip cleared his throat and again attempted the introduction to the Pageant . . .

> "We're glad you came,
> You and the Mrs.,
> to see Eastfield's pageant,
> 'Traditions of Christmas.'"

So far, so good. Mrs. Harmon found herself leaning closer. This was it. She crossed her fingers and silently mouthed the words with Philip. Any moment the Ho-Ho-Hos would come. Maybe, just maybe, he'd get them right.

> "So sit back, relax,
> and enjoy our show,
> merry Christmas to all,
> and Ho-Ho-WooooAAAAAAAAAAAAA!!!!!!!"

Philip never got out that last Ho, thanks to Fluffy, who had chosen that exact moment to make her move. In a flash she leaped out of the shepherdess's arms and jumped right into the middle of Brutus's back. She dug her claws in nice and deep, then took off and ran across the stage. No doubt she figured this would shake things up a bit.

She was right. Sort of. What it actually did was shake things down.

After letting out a tremendous howl of pain, Brutus did what any dog in his position would do. He raced after the cat. I guess he figured it was time for a little dog-to-cat talk. Maybe he was hoping they could sit down and chat over a nice long meal—with Fluffy as the main dish.

Actually, the dog chasing the cat wasn't the problem. It was the wagon that was attached to the dog that was chasing the cat.

And Philip. He'd never been to Disney World, but he was sure that the ride he suddenly found himself on was just as good as any he'd find there. Or at least as scary.

First they shot across the stage to the left. Some children were screaming; others were laughing. Philip wasn't sure what he was doing. He may have been doing both. But one thing was certain . . . he was definitely hanging on. For dear life.

"AHHHHhhhhhhh!" he cried.

As they came to one end of the stage, Fluffy suddenly veered to the right and took off in the other direction. Brutus followed. So did the wagon. And so did Philip.

"OOOOOOoooooo!"

Now they were going the other way—full throttle. Fluffy was howling, Brutus was barking, and Philip . . . well, by now little Philip was definitely into his screaming mode.

"EEEEEeeeeeeee!"

Children jumped out of the way as the wagon swerved and crashed into anything in its path: props, trees, the manger. If it was on the stage, chances are it was being hit by the wagon and sent flying through the air.

Then there were the dancing snowflakes. Philip was the first to see what was about to happen.

"Look out! . . . Watch it! . . . Get out of the way!!"

But the little girls just stood there, frozen. They didn't know which way to go. If they leaped to the right, Fluffy might turn in that direction. If they leaped to the left, Fluffy might head that way.

They didn't have to worry. Fluffy made the decision for them. She did another 180-degree turn and completely missed them. Brutus followed. Maybe the girls would be safe after all, maybe the wagon would also miss them, maybe there would be no catastrophe.

Then again, maybe not.

It was close, but not close enough. As the wagon swung around, it caught the leg of snowflake one. It didn't hit her hard, just hard enough to throw her off balance. Just hard enough to cause her to fall into snowflake two, who fell into snowflake three, who . . . well, suddenly it was a rerun of what happened the last rehearsal. The whole troop was falling like dominoes.

Unfortunately, that was only the beginning. When the last snowflake fell, she landed on one of the towering pieces of scenery at the edge of the stage. It was called a flat. And it was surrounded by several other flats just as tall.

Everyone looked up in terror as the flat started

to tilt back. Then, as if trying to catch its balance, it leaned forward. Then back. A hush fell over the crowd as the tall flat continued to teeter back and forth, back and forth . . . and then it fell, directly into the flat behind it. Which fell into the flat behind it. Which fell into the flat behind it.

Once again it looked like someone was playing a giant game of Topple the Dominoes. Only this time, it wasn't dominoes or even snowflakes coming down, it was the entire set of the Christmas pageant.

Everyone watched in stunned horror as the set disintegrated before their eyes. Nicholas, Louis, Mrs. Harmon. Even little Fluffy—cute little Fluffy who had hopped to safety onto a fire-hose box and was now calmly licking her paws—watched with a certain interest.

Finally the last flat fell with a mighty "K-thwump!"

Now everything was totally leveled. You could even see the concrete wall at the back of the stage. For a long time it was very quiet. Then all eyes slowly turned to Mrs. Harmon.

"Well," she said, clearing her throat. "That was, uh . . . interesting." Then forcing her best smile she added, "All right, everybody, take five."

The crowd started to move off. But, realizing that it might take more than five minutes (more like five weeks) to fix the damage, Mrs. Harmon cleared her throat again. Everybody came to a stop. Now she was going to tell them the truth. Now, no matter how tough it was to take, she'd give it to them straight. "Ah . . ." she stalled. Then suddenly forcing another grin, she said, "Better make that ten."

44

A few minutes later, Nick was hanging around backstage when he heard the following conversation.

"So you're telling me we have no third wise man?" It was Mrs. Harmon's voice. She was on the other side of the flat talking to the principal, Mr. Oliver.

Now, it's not like Nicholas was eavesdropping or anything like that. But when it's your teacher and your principal, and they're talking only three feet away, and you really want to hear what's going on . . . well, it's hard not to kind of overhear some of what's being said. In fact, it's hard not to kind of overhear every word.

"I didn't say he wouldn't be here for sure," Mr. Oliver corrected. "I just think you need to know Derrick is having some very serious problems at home right now."

"I'm sorry to hear that," Mrs. Harmon said. And you could tell by the tone of her voice that she really was sorry. Not for the sake of the pageant, either, but for Derrick.

Mr. Oliver let out a long sigh that seemed to say he was sorry, too. The two turned and started to walk away. As they walked, their conversation grew fainter and fainter.

But Nicholas had heard what he needed to hear. Derrick Cryder had ruined his day again. Only this time he hadn't done it by being a bully. This time he'd done it by being someone in need. Someone who, as his mother had pointed out, needed the love of the Lord.

It was Nicholas's turn to sigh. Why? Why, whenever he turned around, did he keep seeing Derrick in need? What was going on? Why couldn't he just get him out of his mind? I mean, it wasn't like Nick could do anything to help Derrick. The only help Nick had ever been to Derrick was to serve as his punching bag.

Still . . . Derrick seemed to be in Nick's thoughts constantly, along with the feeling that he should help. Somehow, some way, he should tell Derrick what his mom had said about God's love. He should let him know that whatever was going on, he didn't have to go it alone. But how? Nicholas wasn't Billy Graham. He was just a kid. Surely God would find someone else to talk to Derrick.

Wouldn't he?

"So what do you say, Bucko?"

Yes, it was I, the Thundering Thespian. I was still set on saving Nicky boy's little show. It had just taken longer than I had planned. Getting a new pair of wings drawn is no easy task. But here they were—right off the drawing board. I had flown over from the sketch pad in Nick's backpack with my new flappers, eager to show them off. But when I noticed my pet protégé's furrowed brow, I knew he was pondering another ponderous problem.

"Nice flying," Nick mumbled, barely paying attention. *"I hope this is a nonstop flight."*

"No, no, I don't mean my flying—we know that's great—I mean Derrick. What are we going to do about Derrick?"

"I don't know," Nick groaned. *"Maybe someone should talk to him. You know, find out what's wrong . . . that kinda thing."*

I dipped to the right and made a perfect two-point

landing right on Nicky boy's shoulder. You know the spot—the place in all those old cartoons where the "good conscience" speaks to the hero. I figured, hey, I'm wearing angel wings, why not give it a shot?

"What are you going to say to him?" I whispered quietly in his ear.

"Me!" Nicholas practically jumped. He hated it when I could read his mind like that. But, hey, as his very own cartoon creation and part time alter-ego, that came with the territory. "McGee," he continued, "what could I tell him?"

"I don't know," I said, starting to grin. "But it's Christmas. I bet you'll think of something."

"Look." Nick was already on his feet searching for excuses. "I don't . . . I don't even know where he is, OK?"

"Right," I agreed. "'Course you could always start off by checking his home."

Nicholas frowned again.

"No way! Go to his home? Absolutely not. No way, no how, are you ever going to see me at Derrick Cryder's home!"

I smiled, fluttered my wings, and took off for his sketch pad. "Sure thing, Bub," I called. "Let me know when we get there. I still got a few feathers to preen."

FIVE
A Little House Call

Nick wasn't sure how he got to the apartment building where Derrick Cryder lived—or even exactly why he was there. All he knew was that it had something to do with what McGee had said, something to do with what his mom had said, and something to do with what God wanted.

Standing outside in the cold, Nick let out a long puff of white breath and watched as it drifted slowly above his head. This was stupid. Insane. Even if he saw Derrick he wouldn't know what to say. In fact, if Derrick saw him he wasn't sure he'd live long enough to say anything.

But he had gone this far, so he might as well finish it. Even if it was the last thing he ever did. Taking another deep breath, he reached for the lobby door and tugged it open. It gave a gritty screech. He slipped in and pulled it shut behind him as it gave another awful screech.

To call the room a lobby was an exaggeration. It was just a place with worn and chipped floor tiles and a couple of rows of little mailboxes stuffed into the wall. Everything was bathed in a weird yellow light. And the smells . . . they weren't completely suffocating, but they were definitely more lethal than just stale smoke and mildewing carpet.

Then there were the sounds. A baby crying at the top of his lungs. An older guy shouting and yelling in an apartment down the hall. But just a couple of doors away someone was playing "Silent Night." It was kind of pretty. And in a place like this, it was more than a little comforting.

Right next to the mailboxes Nick spotted the directory. It was inside a glass case. White letters on a black board. Well, it used to be black. Now a good portion of it was starting to fade and turn brown from the sun.

Nicholas took a step closer. "Albert, Anderson, Brenner . . . " His mittened hand carefully followed the names down the directory. "Campbell, Cramer, Cryder . . ." There it was. Cryder—apartment 6.

Suddenly, before Nick had a chance to turn and head for what he feared might be his doom, the yelling down the hall grew louder. It was followed by a loud slap and then a muffled cry.

Nick turned just in time to see an apartment door open and a boy rush out, holding his cheek and whimpering. Quickly Nick sucked in his breath. It was Derrick Cryder!

Derrick slammed the door and started down the hall . . . directly toward Nicholas!

At first Nick thought of running, of throwing open the lobby door and racing for his life. But everything was too strange. Derrick Cryder crying?

Then, before he had a chance to get his bearings, it was too late. Before he knew it, Derrick looked his way and their eyes met.

There was a moment of shock for both of them. And embarrassment. Then Derrick gave his eyes a quick swipe, dropped into his famous I'm-a-too-tough-dude slouch, and demanded in a rough voice, "What are you doing here?"

It almost worked. Derrick was almost able to become the Derrick everyone knew and feared. Almost, but not quite. Maybe it was the way his voice cracked. Or maybe it was the look in his eyes . . . that same look Nicholas had seen in the gift shop. A look of fear and hurt.

But it lasted only a second. Immediately Derrick pulled back into the shadows of the hallway so Nick couldn't see him well. But that was OK. Nick wasn't looking. Instinctively he had focused on the chipped tile at his feet. He had seen a Derrick Cryder he was sure no one else at school had seen. And suddenly, surprisingly, Nick wanted to be careful not to embarrass Derrick any further.

"I said," Derrick demanded as his voice grew stronger, "what are you doing here, Squid?"

Well, here goes, Nick thought. *It's now or never.* He opened his mouth. At first nothing came out. He swallowed and tried again. At last a few words started to come.

"Look, I uh . . . umm . . . uh. . . ." Well, only a few words. He cleared his throat and tried again. "That is, uh, we . . . well, we, you know, we missed you."

There! At last he found a handle. Some place to

start. Now if he could just go on from there!
"Yeah," he croaked, growing in confidence. "We missed you at rehearsal today and I just stopped by on my way home to—"

Now he was on a roll. Now he was able to look up at Derrick and . . . oops. He shouldn't have done that. Look up at Derrick, I mean. Because the expression on Derrick's face said he wasn't buying it—any of it. Since when had anyone ever missed him? Since when was anybody ever sorry that he, Derrick Cryder, wasn't around?

Nicholas swallowed again, though by now his mouth was so dry he had little left to swallow. Suddenly, there was a muffled roar of a car approaching outside. Both boys threw a glance toward the street. A dark, souped-up Mustang, missing more than its fair share of paint, rumbled to a stop at the curb. Nick didn't recognize it, but by the tension he saw cross Derrick's face, he knew Derrick did.

Nick took another breath and tried again. It didn't look like he had much time, and he'd better say what he'd come to say . . . whatever it was.

"OK, well, maybe that's not the reason. Well, OK, it's part of the reason, but really, uh, I mean, that is . . . " Enough small talk. Finally it was time to lay it all out on the table. It was tough, but it was what Nicholas really felt. "Derrick, are you all right?"

The sincerity in Nick's voice caught Derrick off guard. But before he had a chance to answer, the Mustang's horn began to blast. Now his attention was split between Nicholas and the Mustang. "What are you really doing here?" he demanded.

Again Nicholas tried to swallow. And again he tried to explain. "It's Christmas." It wasn't much of an explanation, but it was all he had.

"What?"

The horn continued to blast.

"You know, Christmas." Nicholas started fumbling again. "It's supposed to be a time to care about other people and, uh . . . " He looked at Cryder and again he lost his train of thought.

The horn blasted.

Nick tried again. He was going to get through this if it killed him. "I mean, that's the whole reason for Christmas in the first place . . . right?" Things were getting worse and he knew it. Not only was his voice getting weaker, but the horn was blasting louder and Nick doubted he was making any sense at all.

By the look on Derrick's face he knew he was right about the last part. Still, he pressed on. "You know, uh, 'cause God loved us . . . and all that . . . "

He was failing miserably.

". . . sort of . . . "

He was barely making sense, even to himself. Finally the last word came out. But it was more a squeak than a word.

" . . . stuff."

There, he'd said it. Maybe it didn't make any sense but at least he'd said it.

It was no surprise that Derrick looked puzzled and confused. But he also looked like he might have understood . . . just a little. Nicholas wasn't sure.

He never found out. The lobby door suddenly

flew open and there stood Derrick's older friend—the one in the leather jacket that had ripped off the stuff from the gift shop. The blast of cold air from the outside made Nicholas shudder. Then again, maybe it wasn't the cold air . . .

"Let's go, Cryder!" the kid shouted. "We haven't got all night!"

For a moment Derrick also seemed to shudder—and it wasn't because of the cold either. It was because of the menacing grin the boy was wearing, the menacing grin directed right at Nicholas.

"Well, well, well, who do we have here?" The older boy sauntered up to Nick. He was almost a foot taller and probably forty pounds heavier. That wasn't the problem, though. The problem was what Nicholas was wearing.

Now, Nick's not rich. Not by a long shot. But his mom works pretty hard to help the kids look their best—even without much money. Unfortunately, it was this looking their best that had suddenly become Nick's problem. Maybe it was the scarf, or the stocking hat, or even the new mittens. Whatever it was, when the older kid saw Nicholas his face showed what he was thinking: "Spoiled, rich brat." And that definitely meant Nicholas had a problem.

"So . . ." the kid sneered in Derrick's direction. "You plan on bringing your pet freak along tonight?"

Derrick tried his best to be cool. But you could tell by the way his eyes darted around that he knew this kid could be trouble . . . real trouble. "Look, uh . . . " Derrick cleared his throat and

54

motioned toward Nicholas. "He's just a twerp from that stupid play I'm in."

"What?" The kid sounded angry.

Derrick decided to play it safe and bail. "I'm not in it anymore!" he quickly added. "I quit."

For just the slightest second it looked like the kid's face relaxed.

"Come on," Derrick encouraged, "let's get out of here."

But the kid wasn't ready to go. Not just yet. He reached down to the costume Nick was still holding under his arm—the robe and turban from the pageant. Still sneering, he half whispered, half hissed, "Nice dress, girlie."

Nick was paralyzed with fear.

Derrick began to fidget nervously, "Ray . . . "

So the kid's name was Ray. A nice, simple name, Nicholas thought. Straight, to the point, and yet with a certain flair. The type of flair that could spell real disaster.

The sneer slowly disappeared from Ray's face.

Great, Nicholas thought.

But not so great. The sneer was turning into a scowl. Slowly Ray leaned into Nick's face. Not more than four inches separated them. In fact, if Nicholas had been breathing he would have noticed it'd been awhile since the kid had brushed his teeth. But Nick wasn't breathing. In fact, he wasn't doing much of anything . . . except praying.

"I don't know who your friend is," Ray continued to hiss. He was talking to Derrick, but by the glare he was drilling into Nicholas's head, it was pretty obvious he was really addressing him. "But you tell him if I see his spoiled rich face on this side of town again, I'm going to have to kick it all the way back to where it belongs. You got that?"

Both boys got it . . . loud and clear.

"Yeah, yeah," Derrick answered nervously. "Now, come on, let's get out of here before my dad comes."

But Ray was in no hurry. He wanted to make sure he'd put the proper fear into the spoiled rich kid. The look on Nick's face said he had succeeded. He'd succeeded big time!

Just then the horn blasted again, and Ray broke back into that little sneer of his. Nicholas never thought he'd be happy to see it. But that little sneer was better than the scowl. A thousand times better.

Suddenly Ray reached his hand up to Nick's cheek and gave it a little pinch, then a gentle slap. "Ciao," he said with a smirk. Then, to add further insult—"Chicken."

At the moment Nicholas didn't mind the insult. He figured being a live chicken was a lot better than a dead hero.

In an instant Ray turned and threw open the lobby door. Derrick followed without a word. But just before he disappeared out the door he turned back to Nicholas.

"Listen . . . Martin . . . "

The two stood still for just a moment, neither of them sure what Derrick was going to say. Maybe he wasn't going to say anything. But then again . . .

The horn honked and, again, there was Ray's voice:

"C'mon, Cryder!"

Derrick turned and headed out the door into the night. Nicholas watched as the boy got into the back seat of the Mustang with Ray and another kid, and then they squealed off.

Suddenly everything was very quiet.

It had started to snow again.

Nicholas stood in the silence for a long moment. He was stunned and awed by how still everything had become—almost as if the last five minutes had never happened.

There was no other sound, no other movement— just the falling snow. Oh, and one other thing. From down the hall, just a few doors away, came the ending strains to the Christmas carol that had been playing. The music was soft and faint, but there was no missing the final words . . .

"Sleep in heavenly peee-eeace . . .
   Slee-eep in heavenly peace."

SIX
Opening Fright

Finally it was Christmas Eve. Great!

Of course, that meant it also was the night of the big show. Not so great.

To be honest, Nick really wasn't too worried. The fact that he rehearsed his lines all afternoon in front of the hallway mirror, well, that was just good preparation. The fact that he spent almost an hour in the shower, well, that was just good hygiene. And the fact that he completely shellacked his hair with hair spray and used half a bottle of Dad's after-shave . . . well, you never know when a Hollywood talent agent might drop in.

"Let's move, we're going to be late!" Dad hollered for about the tenth time. And for about the tenth time nobody paid attention. How could they? Not when there was still eyeshadow, lipstick, and of course more hair spray to put on.

For years everyone had known that "Let's-move-we're-going-to-be-late!" was just the first warning.

Things weren't critical yet. Not by a long shot. There were still two more warnings to come.

Next would be the famous "I'm not kidding! We have to go!" When you heard that, you knew it was getting close. Still, you'd probably have time to try on a couple more pairs of shoes or, if you were lucky, to slip on one last dress.

It was only when they heard "All right, everyone! We're going, and we're going now!" that the family knew Dad really meant business. There would be no messing around after those words. Once you heard those words you were either heading for the car or staying home.

"I'm not kidding! We have to go!" Ah, the second warning. But for once Nick didn't need a second warning. He already was heading down the stairs to join his dad in the kitchen. In fact, Nicholas had been dressed and bathed and sprayed and combed and ready to go for nearly two hours now. Surely this was further evidence that he wasn't nervous. Petrified, maybe. But not nervous.

Grandma was next to make her appearance. She came down the steps wearing a long dark skirt, a gorgeous white sweater, and a single strand of pearls around her neck.

"Whew! Look at you!" Dad said with appreciation.

Grandma gave a regal nod to her adoring subjects. "So how do you feel, Nick?" she asked. "A little nervous?"

"Naw," Nick said with a shrug. Then, seeing his dad open his mouth, he thought he'd try to beat him to the punch line. But no such luck. "A lot nervous," they said in unison.

Finally Dad turned toward the stairs to call out his third and last warning. "All right, everyone! We're going, and we're going now!"

Immediately there was a loud stampede upstairs. It sounded like a herd of wild buffalo—but it looked like Sarah, Mom, and little Jamie charging down the stairs at the same time. Dad threw Nick a grin. Did he know how to get his family in gear or what?

The three reached the bottom of the steps and raced for the coat rack where they threw on their hats, coats, and scarfs. Dad was still smiling as he opened the door and watched his herd gallop past.

As Jamie moved by, she stuck something out for her brother.

"What's this?" Nicholas asked.

"If you really mess up, you can wear it home."

Nicholas carefully unfolded it. It was a ski mask! What a comfort to know his little sister had such confidence in him.

By the time the family arrived at the auditorium, most of the best seats were already taken. With a little luck (and the fact that most of the ushers were guys who had a crush on Sarah), the Martins managed to find a few good seats in the middle section. Of course, there were the usual hassles of sitting in the middle . . . like climbing over a million and a half feet. But finally they were all seated and ready for the show.

Well, almost. It seems Dad had forgotten something. "I'll be right back," he said as he rose to his feet. Of course, everyone was a little put out as, once again, he had to crawl all over those million and a half feet.

But Dad had to go backstage and tell Nicholas something very important . . .

Backstage was a zoo. Literally! Everywhere you looked there were either live animals, stuffed animals, or people dressed up like animals. In fact, when Dad first poked his head around the flat, it looked more like Noah's ark than the birth of Christ. At last he found his son and called to him.

"Nicholas!"

Nick was standing beside Louis. Both boys were in their wise-man costumes. There was no sign of the third wise man.

"Nicholas!" This time Dad called a little louder.

"Oh," Nick answered. "Hi, Dad." Both Nick and Louis crossed toward him to see what was up.

"Listen," Dad said, pouring a small handful of quarters into Nick's hands. "Here's your allowance. Now everything's set. After the performance I'll take the rest of the family over for some yogurt. That way you can go out and get the music box for Mom. She'll never know a thing. But come straight home."

Nicholas eagerly accepted the money and broke into a grin. With the worries of the pageant and Derrick Cryder, he'd almost forgotten about the music box. "Sure thing," he beamed. "Thanks!"

Dad nodded and started back toward the auditorium. Then, remembering his manners, he turned and hoarsely whispered, "Break a leg, you guys!"

Louis spun around in concern. "What?" But he was already gone.

"Break a leg," Nick repeated.

Louis still didn't get it.

"In the theater it means, like, 'good luck.'"

"In this show," Louis sighed, "it's, like, a possibility."

"All right, places everybody . . . places." It was Mrs. Harmon, once again doing what she did best—clapping and pretending to be happy. But if you looked closely into her eyes you could see that maybe, just maybe, Louis had a point.

A hush fell over the audience as the lights dimmed. The way everybody leaned forward in their seats you would have thought it was opening night on Broadway. Of course, those were parents in those seats. And it was their children up on that stage. So, in many ways, it was more important than any Broadway opening night.

The spotlight came up and focused on little Philip, nervously standing in his sleigh. He was holding the reins to Brutus, the red-nosed dogdeer, and he was looking more than a little frightened. But old Brutus wasn't going anywhere. And, whether he knew it or not, little Philip was about to give the performance of his life.

With a deep breath he began . . .

> "We're glad you came,
>   You and the Mrs.,
> to see Eastfield's pageant,
>   'Traditions of Christmas.'"

So far, so good. But now came the tricky part. As Mrs. Harmon watched from backstage, she crossed her fingers, her toes, her legs, and anything else there was left to cross.

Suddenly there was a commotion behind her. She turned and spotted Derrick Cryder arriving . . . complete with his robe and turban. Without a word he moved past her to join the other two wise men who were standing in the nativity scene, waiting for the curtain to rise.

"Glad you could make it," Mrs. Harmon whispered as he passed.

Without missing a beat he answered, "Somebody said you're giving fewer quizzes the rest of the semester."

Mrs. Harmon had to smile. She knew exactly what he meant. She had blackmailed him by threatening to flunk him. Now he was blackmailing her by showing up! The kid obviously had a future in big business.

Nick watched with pleasure as Derrick joined him. For the first time he could remember, Nicholas was actually happy to see Derrick. He wanted to say this, to tell Derrick how glad he was that he made it . . . but he didn't say a word. It would have only embarrassed and angered Derrick. It would have only gone against his code of ultra-cool-hood.

Instead, both boys prepared themselves for their entrance. The curtain was about to rise. Little Philip was already in the second part of his speech . . . the critical part . . .

> "So sit back, relax,
>   and enjoy our show,
> merry Christmas to all,
>   and Ho-Ho-Ho!"

With that, the little guy gave Brutus' reins a flick and the megadog trotted off as gentle as you please.

It was perfect! Wonderful! Sensational! And the audience didn't hesitate to show their approval. Immediately they broke into cheers as the little boy and the big dog with cardboard antlers headed off.

Now it was time for the nativity scene.

The curtain slowly rose and the audience grew very quiet. There before them was one of the most beautiful nativities they had ever seen. Everything was there: the stable, the animals, the shepherds, the three wise men, Joseph and Mary, and, of course, the manger where the baby Jesus lay.

But it was more than just the scenery and actors that made the moment so special. There was something else. As everybody on stage and in that auditorium turned their attention to the tiny crib, a gentle sense of awe and wonder began to ripple through them.

For a moment—just a moment—they really thought about Christmas, what it means. Sure, it is a time of Santa Clauses and reindeer, Christmas pageants and Christmas gifts, tree decorating and snowflakes (dancing or otherwise). But slowly it dawned on everyone in that auditorium that Christmas is a season of something more . . . of something greater.

A soft spotlight came up on the stage and Nicholas quietly stepped forward. He was about to deliver his lines. Like the scene itself, the lines suddenly took on a deeper meaning. They were more than just words now. They were the whole reason for the evening—the whole reason for Christmas. . . .

"That night some shepherds were in the fields outside the village, guarding their flocks of sheep."

Nick's voice was strong and steady. He stumbled over an occasional word, but nobody seemed to care. Everyone was more interested in what he was saying than in how he was saying it.

"Suddenly an angel appeared among them, and the landscape shone bright with the glory of the Lord. They were badly frightened."

There wasn't a sound in the auditorium. It was as if everyone was watching and listening to the story for the very first time. Maybe some of them were.

"But the angel reassured them. 'Don't be afraid!' he said. 'I bring you the most joyful news ever announced, and it is for everyone!

"'The Savior—yes, the Messiah, the Lord—has been born tonight in Bethlehem! How will you recognize him? You will find a baby wrapped in a blanket, lying in a manger!' Suddenly, the angel was joined by a vast host of others—the armies of heaven—praising God:

"'Glory to God in the highest heaven,' they sang, 'and peace on earth for all those pleasing him.'"

Nick practically shouted the last few lines. It was true. Not only had Jesus come to save people, but he also came to give them peace. Not peace from wars and battles . . . but a peace inside their hearts, a peace deep inside where it really counted, a peace available to everyone . . . "For *all* those pleasing him"!

Everybody was moved by that last phrase. Especially Derrick. It really seemed to touch him. I mean, if there was anyone who needed peace—if there was anyone who needed to know he was loved—it was Derrick Cryder.

That probably was why, as Nick turned to walk back to his place, he clearly saw Derrick reaching up and brushing a tear from his eye.

SEVEN
Confrontation

Two hours later Nick was standing inside the little gift shop. The sign on the door said "Closed," but the shopkeeper had been listening for Nicholas's knock.

It had been a perfect night. Philip had been perfect. Brutus had been perfect. In fact, the whole pageant had been perfect. Then, to top it off, Derrick Cryder had shown up! It couldn't get much more perfect.

Now the shopkeeper was behind the counter. Once again she was lifting the music box from the shelf and setting it before him. Only this time it would never return to the shelf. This time it was going home to Nicholas's mom.

Carefully he ran his hand over the intricate carvings of the glass lid. Gently he opened it and listened as the box began to play. The chiming of the "Carol of the Bells" was just as haunting and stirring as ever. Nicholas looked up to the weathered old lady and grinned.

"I'll get you a box," she said, smiling.

Yes, it was a perfect Christmas.

Not far away, in a dark alley, a hand suddenly grabbed Derrick by the shirt and threw him against a cyclone fence. The fence rattled loudly, which set a couple of dogs barking.

"Where were you?" The snarled question came from Ray, Derrick's "friend." Ray and one of his pals towered menacingly over Derrick. They were lit only by the Mustang's headlights as it idled noisily nearby.

Derrick tried to move, but Ray pinned him hard against the fence. "You know we needed a twerp to squeeze under the gate of that warehouse!"

"I was, uh . . . " Derrick tried to stay cool, but with little success.

"Hey, look at this!" the other kid shouted.

Derrick froze.

They had spotted his costume from the pageant lying on the ground. It had fallen out of his arms when Ray had thrown him against the fence.

The sneer on Ray's face grew deeper. Now he knew where Derrick had been. "You were play-act-ing with your stinkin' rich friend, weren't you?"

"I, uh . . . "

"Weren't you?" His hold on Derrick grew tighter. So tight the boy could barely breathe. Derrick tried to explain but all that came out were gargled gasps.

Ray pressed harder. *"Weren't you?"*

Finally Derrick nodded. That was all it took. With one powerful move Ray threw him across the

alley—slamming him hard against a garbage dumpster. The dogs barked louder.

"Listen, slime!" Ray was breathing hard now. In the cold air, his breath spewed in great white plumes. "I let you tag along, even though you're just a dumb punk. But now, after hanging around that little geek, you think you're too good for us. Is that it?"

"Ra—"

"Is that it?"

Once again Ray grabbed Derrick and jerked him to his feet. Only this time he flung him several feet into the air. Derrick landed hard on the Mustang's fender. He gave a loud "Ommph" as all the air rushed from his lungs. But he had no time to feel the pain. Ray was coming at him slowly, and by the look on his face it would be for the last time. . . .

"Ray," he croaked.

"Go on. Get outta here." Ray's voice was low and quivering. He meant business. "Get outta my sight."

Derrick scrambled to his feet.

"I said, get outta here!"

Derrick needed no further invitation. Immediately he turned and stumbled down the alley.

"But if I see you or that punk friend of yours again . . . you're history!"

The last words echoed up and down the alley as Derrick rounded the corner and headed out into the street.

For the last time Nicholas heard the little bell above the shop door jingle as he closed it. It was colder outside than he remembered, but it was also more beautiful. Somehow the chill made everything more vivid, more alive. The street decorations seemed to twinkle more brightly. The carolers a few doors down sang more cheerfully. Even the bell from the Salvation Army Santa across the street rang more clearly.

All that and it was starting to snow again.

Yes, it was a perfect Christmas Eve. The most perfect ever.

Nicholas carefully stuffed the treasured gift under his arm, adjusted his scarf, and started on his way. Inside his head he could still hear the melody from the music box. Already he could see the look on his mother's face when she opened it. She'd be smiling, of course. But there would also be tears. Even that would be perfect.

The cassette player throbbed as Ray's partner swung the car onto the street. Ray was still angry. Real angry. What business did Derrick have hanging out with rich kids, anyway? They could have made good money by hitting that warehouse. But no, Derrick had to be in some stupid play with some rich brat.

Ray hated anyone who was, or appeared to be, rich. He was sure that everything he never had somehow had gone to them. He couldn't prove it, but all that money and all that "good life" had to go somewhere. And since he always had so little and they always had so much . . .

That was OK, though. Ray would show them. He would show them all.

Nicholas turned the corner and headed for home. It was still snowing and the "Carol of the Bells" was still chiming merrily inside his head.

Half a block away, the Mustang's headlights caught the unmistakable form of Nicholas Martin, bouncing for home. Ray was the first to spot him. "Well, well, well," he said in a soft, dangerous voice, "what do we have here?"

"Turn right," Ray quietly growled to his friend. "Circle around."

The driver punched the gas and the Mustang squealed off around the corner.

Nicholas continued down the street. In less than twenty minutes the family would all start to open their presents. Soon his mom would be opening the best gift he had ever given. Of course, he'd be receiving gifts, too. But somehow, for Nicholas, this year the receiving wasn't quite as important as the giving.

In the next alley, not more than fifty feet ahead of Nicholas, the driver shut off the Mustang's engine and turned out its lights. Now there was only the sound of crunching gravel as the dark machine coasted to a stop.

The door opened. There was no missing the distinct form of Ray's leather jacket as he quietly shut the door and headed off.

Nick was thinking of Derrick. He had failed in trying to tell Derrick about Christmas and God's love and everything. He had failed miserably. But for some reason the guy had still showed up at the pageant. Why? Maybe it was Mrs. Harmon's threat about flunking him. Still . . . And what about that tear Nicholas had seen in Derrick's eye when he had finished his speech?

That had to mean something.

Without a sound Ray pressed against the wall. He had found a place where the shadows were so dark and so deep that he could completely disappear into them. Only the white clouds of breath above his head gave away his presence. His breathing was slow and controlled. He knew exactly what he would do. Nicholas was less than fifteen feet away.

For a second Nicholas slowed. The prized gift he had kept under his arm was starting to slip. He quickly took it in his other hand and started off again.

Then it happened.

Suddenly Nick was yanked into the darkness. Suddenly and violently. Before he could yell, before he even knew what hit him, he was sailing through a black void. He landed in what felt like a heap of boxes. But it wasn't the boxes that hurt. It was the hard metal garbage cans under those boxes. In an instant he and the cans went clattering to the ground. And, in an instant, Nicholas's head hit the pavement . . . hard.

But just before he landed, almost as though in a dream, he caught sight of the music box as it flew from his hands. In slow motion he saw it sliding across the frozen asphalt. He heard the sickening sound of wood and glass scraping against gravel and pavement.

And then he hit.

It still seemed like a dream—or like he was float-ing underwater and the music box was playing above him somewhere, soft and muffled. Then the sound grew sharper . . . along with the pounding in his head. The music box *was* playing. Only it was playing somewhere in the alley. Somewhere in that cold, frozen night it was chiming out its haunting little melody.

Nicholas lay stunned. He still wasn't entirely sure where he was or what had happened. Then he saw it . . . a large, dark form. It was moving. And it was moving toward him. It was impossible to make out who it was. There was only the silhou-ette of a large boy wearing a large leather jacket.

Nick tried to move, to get his bearings. But he couldn't find his legs. Everything was still too weak and blurry. He tried to call out, to say some-thing, anything. But no words would come.

The silhouetted form was much closer now. Giant puffs of white breath were billowing from its mouth.

And then he spoke. "How was the play, girlie?"

Nicholas froze, a shock of terror jolting though him. Even in his bleary state, he recognized the voice—and it sounded meaner and more menacing than ever before.

Again Nick tried to move, but his legs would not obey.

Now the hulking form was nearly on top of him, and Nick heard a vicious little chuckle as two large hands reached out to grab him, bunching Nick's coat collar around his neck—

Suddenly, from out of the blue, another form appeared. It smashed into the first as if shot from a cannon. Together the two shadows tumbled onto the frozen asphalt with grunts and cries of pain. Then they began to slug it out.

Nick tried to rise for a better look. But it felt like a giant ball bearing was inside his head, crashing into the sides of his skull whenever he tried to move. Then there were his legs. They were no closer to obeying his commands than before. All he could do was watch the flurry of fists and legs.

The cussings and cursings and stifled yells grew louder. Whoever this newcomer was, he certainly was giving Ray a run for his money. Suddenly the shadows were up. But only for a second before they fell back down, skidding painfully across the gritty pavement. Bloody knees and elbows pumped and kicked.

"Hey! You there!" It was a voice of a neighbor, a passerby. But the forms ignored it.

"I'm calling the cops!"

As quickly as the fight had started, it was over. A torn and ragged Ray slowly rose over his victim. Apparently he had won, but by the swelling and cuts across his face, it looked like it had been close. He hovered over his defeated opponent a moment, swaying unsteadily. Then he spat on the ground, turned, and staggered down the alley.

Nick watched as Ray's silhouette disappeared. The Mustang roared to life, was thrown into reverse, and squealed backward out of the alley.

Suddenly everything grew quiet. The only sound was the music box as its fragile melody slowly wound down.

With the greatest of effort, and despite the ball bearing still crashing in his head, Nicholas finally managed to sit up and focus his eyes. It was difficult to see because of the shadows—and because of his cut and swollen face. But there, lying on the ground not ten feet away from him, was Derrick Cryder.

Derrick slowly began to stir to life. Groaning slightly, he lifted himself up on his elbows and looked at Nick. For a moment, the boys looked at each other—neither one entirely certain what had happened.

And somewhere nearby, the music finally stopped.

EIGHT
New Beginnings

"And when I saw him thumpin' on the Squid, er
. . . Nick, here—I mean, before I knew it, I was in
there punching away."

The Martin car cut through the thin layer of
snow that had accumulated on the hospital park-
ing lot. To be safe, Mom and Dad had thought it
best to have both boys checked out at the E.R.
But after X-rays, a little poking, and a little prob-
ing, the doctor said everything was OK. Except for
a few bruises and a couple gashes, everything was
just fine.

At first, when they got the phone call, the folks
had had quite a scare. But now everything was set-
tling back to normal. Well, as normal as Nick's life
ever got. Right now, both Nick and Derrick were in
the back seat, reliving what had happened . . . for
the umpteenth time. And each time the story got a
little bigger and a little better.

"But the neatest thing is," Nicholas exclaimed,

"Derrick never would have done that for me before. I mean, stepping in and helping like that."

"No way," Derrick agreed. "I wouldn't have done that for nobody."

There was a moment of silence as both boys digested this cold, hard truth.

"The weird thing is," Derrick finally continued, "I really don't know why I did it this time. It's like . . . " Again he fell silent for a moment as he tried to figure it out. "It's like something's happening." Another long moment passed. At last he gave a shrug. "I don't get it. I don't get any of it."

In the front seat Mom and Dad exchanged glances. For months they had heard about Derrick Cryder, and for months they had told Nick there was hope for anyone, even Derrick.

Dad was the first to speak. "It sounds like you're starting to go through some changes."

Derrick glanced up at him. The man was right. Of course, Derrick was too cool to admit it. But the look on his face said he wanted to hear more— lots more. Dad obliged.

"And not just you," he continued. "I mean, the same thing happened with Nick. I bet the last thing in the world he wanted to do was to visit your place the other night."

"Boy, you got that right," Nicholas agreed, perhaps a little too quickly.

Derrick shot him a look. It was Nicholas's turn to give a shrug. Hey, at least he was being honest.

"But," Dad continued, "there was something stronger at work than just what you two wanted."

Now he had both boys' interest. It was true—

neither one of them really wanted to do what he did. I mean, going to Derrick's apartment was certainly not Nick's idea of a good time. And Derrick could have thought of a hundred better things to do than getting creamed by Ray just to save Nick's neck. And yet, somehow, they both wound up doing the harder thing—the better thing. Why?

"It's love," Mom finally said. "God's love."

Normally Derrick would have scoffed at the idea. But after tonight, well, who knows. Anything was possible. So instead of scoffing, Derrick just listened.

Mom and Dad carefully began to explain to Derrick how much God really loves him—how much he really loves everyone. They described how God wants to be our friend, but how we've all turned our backs on him and disobeyed. Then, even more carefully, they explained how Jesus came to earth to take the punishment for that disobedience.

"You mean this Jesus guy got beat up, and spit on, and killed . . . just so he could take the rap for all my crumminess?" Derrick asked.

"You got it," Dad said.

"Everything?"

"Everything."

"So . . . what's in it for him?"

"Not a thing."

Derrick whistled. This was getting interesting.

"The only thing he wants," Mom added, "is to be your Boss and your Friend."

"Yeah, right," Derrick smirked. "Me, friends with God."

"Why not?" she challenged.

Derrick looked at her in surprise. This *was* getting interesting. Why not, indeed?

"'Cuz . . . well, well, I'm just not good enough," Derrick finally stuttered.

"None of us are," Mom said.

Then, almost before he knew it, Nick had his mouth open. Normally he wouldn't have much to say on the subject. I mean, Jesus and God and all that—it was hard stuff to talk about. Especially to someone who's been spending the school year making your life miserable. Yet he and Derrick had been through so much together, and, well . . . it sure looked like God had gone out of his way to bring Derrick this far. The least Nick could do was to give him a little hand.

"That's the whole reason Jesus came," he began. "Because we're not good enough."

Derrick turned to him a little surprised. But Nicholas was on a roll and wasn't stopping.

"You see, it doesn't matter how good a person is or how often they go to church or anything like that. It's whether or not they want Jesus to take the blame for all the wrong they've done."

"Well, who wouldn't?" Derrick challenged.

"Got me," Nick agreed. "It'd be pretty stupid not to."

"Real stupid," Derrick said. "But if a person did that, wouldn't they have to start, like you said, letting him be their Boss and doing good and stuff?"

"That's true." It was Dad's turn to answer. "But letting God be your Boss and doing good, that would all start coming naturally—as naturally as your stepping into that fight to save Nicholas."

80

A silence fell over the car as the four drove through the night. Derrick was obviously thinking, and thinking hard. So was Nicholas. He had never talked to anyone so boldly about Jesus. He had never asked anyone if they wanted to become a Christian. But there was a first time for everything.

Another long moment passed. Then, finally, after taking a moment to find his voice, Nicholas asked the question. It wasn't loud and, to be honest, it really wasn't all that bold. In fact, it was kind of shaky. But it was still being asked.

"Derrick . . . is this, like, something you might want? You know, to be friends with God and stuff?"

Derrick turned to him. The two looked at each other for a long moment.

NINE
Wrapping Up

Yes-siree-bob. Ol' Nicky boy was right. It was one perfect Christmas. But it wasn't perfect because of the snow, or the pageant, or even because of all the neato-keen gifts I managed to haul in.

That Christmas was perfect because Derrick and Nick both got another kind of gift. A real gift. The gift of God's love. Derrick's gift came when he decided he did want to be friends with God, to let God be his Boss. And Nicholas's gift was that God used him to help give Derrick his gift. So, if you ask me, both of the guys won, and in a big way. It's like I always say: that's what Christmas is really all about . . . God giving us his greatest gift: his Son, Jesus Christ.

Of course, the Martins invited Derrick home that Christmas Eve. And, of course, Derrick refused. He had too much to think over. I mean, let's face it, the guy had made a pretty big decision. But he promised he would swing by the house sometime before school started up. After all, he had questions. Lots of 'em.

And, just in case you were wondering, Nick managed to retrieve Mrs. Mom's music box. It was pretty chipped and scratched by the time he gave it to her. But somehow those chips and scratches made it all the more valuable.

"Oh, Nicholas," she said as she took it in her hands.

But that was all she got out before the waterworks started. And we ain't talking small-time sniffles, either. I mean, you would've guessed we'd sprung a water main, the way the tears were flowin'.

Then, when she opened the lid and the music started playing . . . well, you could kiss any dry eye in the house good-bye. Everybody was getting into the act. Even yours truly.

"What's goin' on?" I finally managed to sniff between bawling attacks. "Somebody peelin' onions around here?"

But before Nick could give me one of his snappy comebacks, ol' Mom had thrown a lovelock around him so tight he could barely breathe. Then, before you knew it, the whole family joined in. Suddenly I was swept up into this giant hug-in. I couldn't move, I couldn't talk. And pretty soon I could feel my colors starting to rub off on their clothes.

Oh well, there are probably worse ways for a cartoon character to go than being hugged to death.

And speaking of going . . . I see by the giant watch being scrunched into my face from Mr. Dad's arm that it's time to split. So, good tidings, good cheer, ta-ta, and Merry Christmas! (Unless of course you happen to be reading this in February, when it's Happy Valentine's Day . . . or in April, Happy Easter . . . or in May, Happy Mother's Day . . . or in June, Happy Father's Day . . . or in July, Happy . . . oh well, I think you get the picture.)

So, Happy Whatever, and we'll catch all you Buckoes and Buckettes a little later.